HOW TO PLAN FOR A SUCCESSFUL SUMMER CAMP:

7 Ideas On How to Plan for summer camp.

CHRISTINA R. GLOVER

This Book is dedicated to God Almighty, the Alpha and Omega, my defender, my backbone, the one who is, who was, and who is to come. The one who has forever been good to me.

Copyright Page

Table of Contents

INTRODUCTION

If you're considering arranging a camp, you're probably wondering what you'll need. Before embarking on your vacation, write a list of everything you believe is necessary. You must buy specific items for everyone, such as food or drink, and you must do so wisely to avoid quarrels and issues. If you opt to bring food from home, consider things that are easy to transport, such as sandwiches, dried fruit, fruit, vacuum-packed cold cuts, juices, soda cans, and so on. If you prefer to cook more, use spaghetti or breaded steaks and pack them in a sturdy lunch box, avoiding sauces at all costs. Remember to bring disposable plastic cups, plates, utensils, and napkins.

Individually, each member of the group is required to bring a set of goods and resources suitable for carrying out the camp. This type of activity necessitates the use of a tent, sleeping bag, and mat. Remember to bring a lamp or flashlights, bug repellent, plastic waste bags, and a canteen. If you have one, you can carry it with you and cook while camping. Don't forget to bring comfortable shoes, a change of clothes, basic hygiene supplies, and a first-aid kit.

CHAPTER ONE

<u>The camping destination</u>

The destination must be determined before the vacation can begin. You must remember that you cannot camp anywhere and that there are ideal and suited settings and places for you to camp comfortably and without risk. However, you might hunt for a nearby or distant area to appreciate nature wherever you wish.

Before settling on a vacation, gather your friends and discuss all of the possibilities that suit your interests and preferences; you can choose a location on the beach or in the mountains. You must keep in mind that it must be a location where excursions or other activities can be carried out to make the trip more enjoyable.

What do you need for camping, and how do you organize a camp?

- **Useful camping advice**

It is vital to consider some beneficial tips before camping since it is not as simple as pitching the tent and placing it anyplace. We provide you with the following list of requirements for the camp's location:

- **Base in designated areas or natural regions.**

- **To protect everyone's safety, avoid places with trees.**

It is relatively common to select flat terrain. However, keep in mind that the earth may flood more easily during rainstorms. It is best to look for a location with a slight incline. Look for a wind-sheltered location. It is best to position the tents perpendicular to the wind.

Try to identify the plants in your surroundings. Many are prickly, stinging, or deadly, so you should avoid sleeping near them. The camp's location is recommended to be clean, with no pebbles, branches, stones, or other objects that interfere with rest. It is advised to have access to a river or drinking water nearby.

Keep fires and bonfires to a minimum. If done, tidy up the area to avoid a fire. Remember to clean up after yourself and leave the natural space in good condition.

CHAPTER TWO

8 Tips for Creating a Memorable Summer Camp Program

Are you thinking of starting a summer camp program? Here are some ideas for making your summer camp program more enjoyable and successful.

You must have a good plan of action if you are planning to start a summer camp or if you are the camp's coordinator. The place must be determined. You must decide whether the summer camp will be an overnight session or a day program. If it is an overnight program, hundreds of factors must be considered. Everything must be taken care of, from the housing to the daily meals. If you are planning a daytime program, you will need to employ a transportation service, as well as volunteers. Furthermore, the amount to be collected from participants must be calculated. It's time to take real action after you've finished planning such financial and administrative details.

Summer camps are popular among children. They want to have fun, learn new things, and, of course, make new friends! So, aside from the financial and venue aspects, the following considerations can help assure the summer camp's success.

Themes for Summer Camp: You should have a piece in mind when organizing a summer camp. A summer camp theme will inform attendees about the nature of the center. You could, for example, hold a swimming summer camp. The kids who are interested in swimming will attend your camp. If you plan on having a lot of games, you could title it "adventure land" or something like that. Furthermore, an art camp would have a theme such as 'paint the world,' and so on.

Summer Camp Games: If the summer camp is an overnight program, you must keep the children occupied with activities other than the main activity (as in the theme). Plan innovative and enjoyable games. A scavenger hunt, sack race, relays, and other activities are possible. Games are one of the most influential and most accessible ways for children to unwind. They also assist children in becoming acquainted with one another and developing the capacity to work cooperatively.

Allow for Free Time: Kids at summer camp need time to themselves. Make sure to set aside some time for them. This time can be used to establish new friends or to investigate oneself. You may even urge children to write down their impressions of the summer camp or keep a diary of their everyday activities. It is important not to force them to do anything; instead, let them be on their own; if necessary, a few words of encouragement will suffice.

Counselors: Counselors and doctors should be present when planning a summer camp program. If a child is not performing well at camp, he may become homesick or unhappy.

During these moments, a doctor or a counselor can help the child feel at ease. Counselors can also play an essential part in researching children's behavioral patterns, assisting organizers in bringing out the best in a child, and increasing the quality of the summer camp.

A Unique Day: A special day might be planned for your summer camp program. You might host a celebration or something, similar to an annual day at school. You can also arrange a cultural day or a talent show where the students can show off their culture or custom while also learning about different cultures. A talent day would require each youngster to demonstrate their talent, such as playing the guitar, dancing, singing, or drawing.

Art Day: How about organizing an art day? Origami, pottery, painting, and drawing may all be taught to children. You might also decorate the camp in a style that the children desire. You might also organize an exhibition to display the numerous crafts done by children or create a summer camp appreciation wall/string. Gather all the arts and drawings and tape them to the wall, or hang them on a thread with colorful clips.

Adventure Sports: Adventure sports are the most exciting aspect of a summer camp! Plan for rock climbing, river crossing, snorkeling, paragliding, and so on. Of course, you must prepare all of this under the supervision of specialists and organize the necessary equipment for these sports. Please ensure that you do not compel a child to participate in an activity they are afraid of. However, positive remarks to lift the kids' spirits are always appreciated. Even better, give children the choice of doing the work with an adult, which may instill confidence in them to like these sports.

Nature and Science: You can spend a day or two doing science and nature activities. For example, undertake particular tests or walk around the campsite looking up the scientific names of trees. Make this exercise enjoyable and fascinating so that the children do not grumble about it being a study activity. Wordplay is an excellent idea because it is both informative and amusing. Furthermore, if a fun factor is associated with particular items, children tend to recall it more quickly than usual.

CHAPTER THREE

Many people associate summer camps with happy childhood experiences. They can be a place for enrichment whether it's learning a new skill, exploring the arts, or participating in sporting activities or just plain old fun in the sun. Summer camp concepts are so diverse that they can be whatever you want them to be.

Many of the barriers to founding your camp are being removed by technology. You'll be able to swiftly and efficiently design a camp that appeals to both children and parents with the correct technological solutions.

With a bit of imagination and planning, you'll be well on produce an unforgettable experience for young people. We'll go through the legal requirements for getting started and how to set up summer camp registration, price, hiring, activity ideas, and much more. Many of these stages aren't limited to summer camps; they may be used at any camp.

So, how do you go about starting a summer camp?

Plan the logistics. Determine the type of camp you want to run, locate an appropriate location, create a business strategy, and complete all legal procedures and documentation. Create a safe and simple registration process. Using online forms for everything from registration to medical exemptions can help to speed up the process.

Choose a theme and organize your activities around it. Do your homework and get the word out. Understand your target market and create efficient marketing efforts.

Ensure your campers' health and safety. Plan healthful meals, engage janitors or assign jobs, and ensure that the facilities are in working order.

Hire and train employees. Create job descriptions, applications, and policies, as well as employee evaluations.

Gather feedback and stay in touch with campers. Asking kids and their parents for feedback will not only help you enhance your camp, but it will also keep your clients interested long after camp is ended.

What kind of camp do you wish to start?

Answering this question involves some thought and is an excellent moment to assess your goals, talents, and hobbies.

Keep logistical factors in mind. Is your camp going to be a day camp or an overnight camp? Before you can answer these questions, you must evaluate your budget, the environment of your camp, and your staffing situation, as day camps and overnight camps have quite distinct financial issues to keep in mind.

Choose something for which you believe you are uniquely qualified. For example, if you are a musician, you may be able to share your knowledge with a younger generation. Creating a camp based on your skill is a great way to deliver something essential and one-of-a-kind.

It would be best if you also chose a summer camp topic that will thrill you and keep you interested throughout the ups and downs of camp organization. Though establishing a summer camp is simpler than you might think, there is still a significant amount of paperwork to be completed.

You should also be informed of the market in your immediate vicinity. If there are several popular sports summer camps in your area, starting another sports summer camp may not be the most outstanding choice.

Ideally, you want to introduce a fresh summer camp concept to your area. If your community lacks a specific form of summer camp, keep that in mind when brainstorming summer camp ideas. You might construct a form that asks parents what they want their children to learn, what logistical concerns they have, and what they believe is missing from current camp offers.

Maintain an open mind

While many summer camp ideas are likely to be for children, you may be surprised to learn that more and more adult summer camps are springing up, offering adults job enrichment, couples counseling, and other skills and activities appropriate for more mature age groups. A variety of camp ideas can work as long as you approach the situation with imagination and passion. You can make a difference in society with your camp, much like a skating camp.

Making a business plan

Every successful summer camp starts with defined business goals and a step-by-step plan to achieve them. You want a camp that will last. This page will highlight the procedures and discuss the numerous factors in creating a successful summer camp business plan. But, on a broad level, here are a few things to think about when you start your camp:

Market investigation

Before constructing your company plan, you must first understand the market. What are camp goers seeking? What is the demographic in your region? For example, are there a lot of working parents that need to drop their kids off someplace during the day? Are there many parents in the region who support the arts or sports?

What marketing materials do you want to invest in now that you know your market? Who do you want to reach out to? Create a marketing campaign with intriguing content that reaches your target audience. Video, blogs, and other innovative channels to consider as you develop your marketing strategy

How much money do you intend to spend on running your camp? How much will your employees be paid? What is the cost of renting the land you use (if you are renting)? When creating your budget, make sure to consider everything. Small fees can quickly mount up, especially for overnight programs. Pay attention to the specifics make sure every roll of paper towels you'll need to purchase is included. Then, if possible, consult with an accounting firm to ensure that your budget is correct and your accounts are kept up to date.

Pricing and profit objectives how profitable do you anticipate your camp will be? When you evaluate your budget and the future costs, what pricing tier do you believe your camp will fall into? When answering these questions, keep your market in mind to see if pricing your camp at a reasonably high level is a reasonable option.

As you can see, all of these pieces interact with one another. You can't estimate profitability without first completing market research, and you can't decide on price until you know how profitable your camp will be. Working with a business professional while you create your camp is an excellent idea. While business knowledge is required to start a camp, it is unlikely that this is the significant competence of a camp manager. Learn from others and follow the data to ensure you have a long-lasting business plan.

While we've already discussed how digital technologies may help the summer camp creation process, it's important to remember that summer camp still requires an actual venue. While you can utilize digital tools for hunting for potential places, including extensive internet research, you'll still need to get out there and look for a space on your own two feet. Here are some things to consider while searching for the ideal place.

- ***Find a venue that fits your concept, not the other way around***

What amount of outdoor area do you require? What equipment will you require, and how much space will this equipment take? In brief, think about your camp's topic and the activities in which campers will participate. Allow that to influence your space selection rather than picking a space without much thought and bending your camp's plans to fit this space.

- ***Consider the costs***

When selecting a space, you must evaluate both cost and value. For example, if you need to reduce part of your camp activities to afford a specific area, be open to this compromise. Analyze your location from a cost-benefit aspect, just like when looking for a new home or apartment. Perhaps you'll give up some room in exchange for the opportunity to set up a tent in a convenient area.

- ***Is the area suitable?***

You want children and parents to access your camp readily, so it can be in the middle of nowhere, especially if it involves daily drop-off and pick-up of attendees. Because camps are often an excellent alternative for busy, working parents, you want your camp's location to accommodate their hectic schedules. Otherwise, they may choose a camp that is more convenient for them.

- ***Remember the fundamentals***

While it may seem apparent, you should ensure that your camp is in a safe location with enough restrooms and first aid facilities. While it is hoped that this would not be necessary, you will want your camp to be close to a hospital in an emergency. Being close to these basics puts parents at peace, guarantees children's safety, and makes your campers feel more at ease.

Is there anything exceptional about it?

Aside from practical considerations, you want your venue to feel unique. It should appear to be a place where memories will be created. If a room feels "right," you'll typically know. Don't choose a location hastily. Look around, weigh your options, and select a location that will allow your camp to make a difference in the lives of your campers.

- ***Regulations and laws***

Running a summer camp is a significant undertaking. That is why it is critical that you follow all legal procedures and fill out all necessary documentation before opening your camp.

Regardless, you will need waivers, especially if you plan on excursions or day trips. Permission forms signed by parents are also required for day trips and excursions.

Dropdowns, single- and multiple-choice questions, graphics, and other features can be added to forms. Your disclaimers and paperwork can be as detailed as you need them to be, and they can be customized to match your camp's website and brand.

- ***Forms of registration***

Proper camp administration puts everything in order, allowing you to spend less time worrying about paperwork and more time delivering a fun, engaging experience for your campers. The registration form is the first step toward creating an organized atmosphere at your camp.

Online forms also make it simple to keep track of the actual number of applications received without the need for tedious counting. You may then view and sort all of your campers' applications in one spot.

Do you need to compare two applications quickly? Online forms make this simple, allowing you to get applications without having to go through mounds immediately. Saving time by using online forms that are easy to customize, fill out, save, share, classify, and track.

Using a web form can assist you in quickly accepting payments, saving registrant information, and sharing information with your team. This suggests you're ready to accept payments and obtain detailed registrant information simultaneously. All of your data is in one place.

Ready to share your information with your team? Online forms make this easy. You'll connect your registration forms with CRMs, email marketing services, and spreadsheets saving any time.

And don't worry, if you would like to gather signatures or image files for camper IDs, online forms make it easy. Gone are the times of thick files with multiple sheets of paper for ID photocopies, signed consent forms, and registration information. Now you'll have all of that information in one easy-to-navigate place.

Collect emergency contact info, manage records, recruit volunteers, and more with our free online camp management forms. Not all the forms are equivalent. But what kind of information does one need from your campers? That's up to you. Many online forms allow you to customize form fields to get only the knowledge you would like nothing more, nothing less. If you want detailed information for your camp, easy customization can assist you in including valuable fields.

Maybe you're running a music camp and wish to understand which instrument each registrant plays and their skill level. All you would like to try to dodo is customize your forms to gather that information.

CHAPTER SIX

Once you've developed a solid business plan for your camp, confirm you're pricing your centre reasonably. Mind Meld your budget and profit goals, but don't forget to think about the market you're in and, therefore, the affluence of the world where you're drawing potential campers.

One consideration is to cost your camp to the families who will afford it to offset those who can't. Pricing too low sends a message that the camp experience isn't valuable and causes you to lose out on significant revenue opportunities.

- ***Profitability of a camp***

In the previous section, we discussed choosing a camp registration fee. This is often a difficult decision that depends on many factors. Beyond considering the budget, you furthermore may decide how profitable you would like your camp to be. Assuming your centre isn't a non-profit, you'll get to have complex numbers and profit margins — then choose a fee that helps you hit them.

According to a recent ACA survey, camp profitability is on the increase. Half the camps that participated in the survey reported profits, including a median profit value of $90,000 and a 16.2-per cent average profit margin. Though overnight camps attended report less profit, 45 per cent of them were profitable (with 28 per cent reporting a profit of $100,000 or more).

With these numbers in mind, it's essential to recollect that each camp is different, and profit margins tend to vary significantly between centres, no matter type. While day camps tend to post more significant profit margins, their profits can still be volatile. Perhaps the survey's most encouraging takeaway is that yields have been trending positively over the past 12 years since the ACA collected this data. In short, the industry is flourishing.

One of the best expenses of running a camp is staff salaries. This is, of course, a substantial expense. However, it's worth carefully calibrating staff salaries about registration fees so that you'll still pay your staff fairly while fixing your camp to be profitable. As costs add up, you'll get to look elsewhere for revenue sources. Centres have found additional revenue from renting their facilities to others, running programs for college groups, or running adult programming.

Calibrating the length of the camp is additionally crucial for profitability. Maybe you would like to feature more camper days to gather extra money and justify increasing the worth of your centre. You want to consider the expenses that come from running your camp longer and whether this may impact the standard of your centre.

Running a profitable camp helps assure that you'll be ready to maintain your centre for years to return. It also allows you to improve your programming and potentially pay your staff more. Luckily, there's a vast trove of knowledge to assist you in opting for a price and structure that permits your camp to be profitable. And amid it all, it's good to understand that the camp industry isn't the only one that impacts the lives of children it also turns profits.

- ***Benefits of collecting the applications and payments together***

One of the most significant benefits of using a web form for camp registration is the indisputable fact that all the knowledge you would like names, contact information, etc. will be in one place. This extends to payment information too. If registrants use PayPal, Stripe, or other payment software, you'll need knowledge about those accounts.

Suppose you would like to gather subsequent payments during the summer or give refunds; having that payment information in one place makes this process much easier for you and, therefore, the registrant. This is also the case if you're fixing recurring payments for the camper throughout the summer. Keeping application and payment information together allows you to contact the camper if there are any issues with their price. With a web form, this information is accessible, and problems are often solved quickly.

Campers who have a scholarship or a sponsor mean more paperwork for you to stay track of. Storing this information with other camper details helps you stay organized. Keeping all camper information in one place makes the entire process more straightforward and less susceptible to (costly) mistakes.

CHAPTER SEVEN

Now that you've selected a number of the specifics of your camp, it's time to return with a marketing plan. The sell for a centre isn't too hard: you're providing a service for campers and fogeys alike that has the prospect to complement their child's life: physical or academic enrichment, lifelong friendships, and timeless memories. The marketing copy writes itself! Still, you would like to seek out the proper people to plug in and are available with a camp marketing plan that reaches these parents. Here are some ideas:

- ***Market to busy parents***

We've already discussed this a touch, but it bears repeating. Busy parents see camp as an enormous boon. It keeps their children engaged safely while they're at work. Once you zero in on busy parents as your audience, you'll have a neater time deciding which marketing channels to use.

- ***Get a call from the general public***

Consider doing something sort of a free clinic together with your staff that serves a community you'd wish to see at a future camp. Not only will it allow future camps to attach to your team and mission, but it's also an excellent branding boost confirm to bring flyers and printed materials.

And thereon note, confirm who you're trying to draw into your camp is reflected in your marketing materials. As an example, if you'd like equal representation for girls and boys in your centre, having brochures only featuring boys could discourage girls eager to attend.

- ***Pay attention to SEO***

Generally, parents will discover your camp while researching camps online they will rarely go on to your site unless they're returning customers. So it's crucial to optimize your site to realize program traffic. Using specific keywords and phrases that describe your services will help your site rank as high as possible and drive more traffic.

- ***Consider your budget***

If you're starting a replacement camp, you might want to place extra money into advertising to ensure people realize your centre. Since you don't have a stable of returning campers to believe, it'd be real-time to experiment with paid advertising to ensure your centre is exposed in search results. This is especially useful for brand-spanking new camps because you might not have the SEO built to drive tons of organic search traffic.

- ***Develop a branding strategy***

Branding may be a major part of your camp marketing plan. All of your ad materials should convey a uniform tone and aesthetic. More and more successful camps are successful brands. For instance, a camp marketing to serious athletes must be more special than a musical camp aimed toward younger children. This extends to social media also. Create social copy that aligns together with your camp's style.

- *Market year-round*

Your camp may run within the summer, but your marketing plan should run at the least time. This will be as simple as uploading pictures of last summer onto Instagram throughout the year. This helps you stay engaged with past campers, potentially encourage them to return, and keeps your camp visible beyond just the summer months.

What you are doing will depend upon your budget. You'll get to take a while with a financial advisor to work out what proportion you'll spend. Social ads tend to be rather cheap within the grand scheme of things, so investing in social could be an economic thanks to drawing attention. And, like any marketing plan, put money into what works. If placing your camp in camp directories is paying off, it's worth investing and finding more guides. In short, follow the channel that's driving conversions.

- *Marketing options*

When it involves marketing your camp, you've got many options. Social media has been an enormous game-changer for camp advertisements, as social channels tend to be populated by audiences with an interest in summer camps. But ultimately, a holistic plan is best. Use the various marketing channels available social, camp websites, digital ads, physical ads, and in-person meetups and adjust your budget to support the best medium.

Summer camp website directories. Many sites list different summer camps and permit users to filter by camp type, location, etc. Considering the number of centres out there and the intimidating process of zeroing in on just the proper one, these are often an excellent tool for folks trying to find a camp for their child. That's why it's essential to urge in one among these directories.

- ***Digital ads***

While this is often a rather costlier option, having eye-catching digital camp advertisements can go an extended way toward driving attention to your camp. This needs design assets whether this includes your camp's logo, the utilization of images from your campsite, graphic design elements, or some combination of all of the above and individual written copy, like a slogan or concise description of your camp. Using advanced ad software to possess this ad run within the social channels of somebody who may need to look for "summer camps within the Boston area" could assist you in reaching your audience.

- ***Physical ads***

With all those new-fangled advertising options, it's easy to forget how effective an honest physical ad is in drawing attention to your camp. And physical ads are affordable. Designing and printing flyers can cost only a couple of dollars. Then, hanging these flyers up at, say, local schools or libraries can catch the attention of oldsters. They're an excellent thanks to engaging your audience at the highest of the funnel, piquing their interest and inspiring them to find out more.

- ***You were pounding the pavement***

It's obvious: you're the simplest spokesperson for your camp. As a founder, you're the foremost passionate and ultimately qualified to speak up for your centre to interested parties. That's why it's an excellent idea to urge face-to-face as much as possible. Suppose you've got the prospect to go to, for example, schools or rec centres and present your camp at some camp exhibition or summer activities fair. In that case, you'll get to satisfy numerous potential campers and convey your enthusiasm in a face-to-face environment.

Advertising your camp doesn't need to be complicated or prohibitively expensive. What's most vital, especially in the beginning, is trying various advertising methods and studying what works and what doesn't. Then specialize in investing within the channels that drive campers to your site and forget the processes that aren't working.

Summer camps aren't huge multinational companies with eight-figure advertising budgets. Instead, you've got the prospect of making a marketing and branding strategy that feels personal and driven by your enthusiasm for the camp. Using testimonials from past campers, heart-warming imagery from past instalments of your camp (if applicable), and knowledge about you and your background is a good way to convey your camp as a sort of a family one that's hooked on improving the lives of its campers.

CHAPTER EIGHT

- ***Risk management and waiver forms***

The most important thing to recollect when running your camp is the number of trust parents is fixing you and your staff. That's why safety has got to be your number one priority and why you would like to require numerous precautions before getting your camp up and running.

- ***Summer camp parental consent forms***

During the registration process, you would like to urge consent from parents. This will be for the camp generally and specific day trips you've got planned throughout the summer. It's simple: permission slips and consent forms prove that a parent knew about and approved of activity at camp. Say your centre offers physically intense training like zip lining. You would like to form sure that oldsters are aware this activity is occurring before the camp experience, and they grant permission for her child to participate during this activity.

- ***Summer camp medical forms***

A radical medical record of every camper should be provided before your camp begins. These forms provide you with a warning of any allergies or medical conditions that a trailer has so that you'll proceed accordingly for the duration of the camp. As example, if a camper must take a particular medication regularly, you'll confirm that routine is being observed which the trailer is correctly following any medical protocols.

- ***Summer camp release and waiver***

Release forms help protect camps in the case of an accident or other unexpected incident at the centre. They're important legal documents that are key to the healthy operation of a centre. A release form outlines the activities and risks present at the centre. It includes the acknowledgement and assumption of said risks. Release forms are complicated; anyone who runs a camp should be intimately conversant.

As you create your waiver form, certain widgets might be available in handy. For example, you'll get to collect signatures in your document, so using an E-signature widget may be a must. Say you would like the signature of a medical care physician on a medical record. Online forms make it easy to send your document to the acceptable party and quickly collect the signature you would like.

Waivers, releases, and consent forms are often wordy. How are you getting to fit all of that fine print on one online form? Do not worry. The short scrollable terms widget helps you save on vertical space and lets users quickly scroll through the required text. This widget can also easily be configured to suit your form's design. Many (important) readers don't need to get in the way of a nice-looking and easy-to-navigate format.

These are complex documents it's worth carefully creating them and ensuring you're outlining all of the required information (risks, activities, etc.) on the shape and collecting all the signatures you would like. It's not going to be the foremost glamorous or exciting part of the camp management process, but it's arguably of the utmost importance.

You have the medical records and consent. But are you HIPAA compliant? When collecting medical information from potential campers, you must remember and respect privacy laws. The insurance Portability and Accountability Act (HIPAA) found certain safeguards to guard medical data and knowledge and stop it from being exploited. Summer camps must take care when collecting medical forms. You don't want to end collecting your campers' medical information and learn that you haven't been HIPAA compliant.

These forms work on mobile platforms and may be customized to collect your desired knowledge. They will even be integrated into other third-party HIPAA-compliant apps, like Google Sheets and Salesforce. As your campers, or more often, their parents, fill out important medical information, they won't need to worry about whether this sensitive information goes to be mishandled.

CHAPTER NINE

We all know that camp allows children of all ages to get some fresh air, make memories, and meet friends. But developmental psychology experts have conducted studies and learned that the advantages of summer camps might run even deeper.

Five camp benefits for teenagers

Here are a couple of the social development benefits of camp:

- ***A time for unconstrained creativity***

Camp is many students' first opportunity to make things art, written work, etc. without stress about grades. The fact that camps have a sense of leisure gives many students the liberty and willingness to undertake new things and reach new creative heights. Most easily, it gets students creating. Rather than playing video games, camp helps them find out how to form their own computer game. Getting out of the house and into camp is often an excellent chance to fight teenage internet addiction, an increasingly urgent problem in social psychologists' eyes.

- ***A change of pace for unique learners***

Some students struggle in class. Whether it's an inability to sit still, a singular learning style, or behavioural issues, life in a classroom isn't always the perfect learning environment for a student. That's why camps are often so beneficial for those students who don't always thrive in a traditional academic atmosphere. Some camps are often remedial, presenting information a student might not have absorbed well in class or they will spark a replacement interest. This building material doesn't appear in many grammar school curricula. Camps are often fresh air for college kids who want to find out but sometimes struggle in class.

- ***Building friendships supported interests***

Many childhood friendships spring from serendipitous twists of fate, like hitting it off with a child who lives down the road or sits next to you in algebra class. Camp presents the chance to satisfy friends in a new way and build a relationship around common interests. While any friendship is great for a toddler, one based around like-minded passions (e.g., music, programming, etc.) offers the likelihood of the latest intellectual depth. Having discussions with another child helps kids develop mature communication skills and aids in adolescent social development. And there are many stories about children at music camp forming a band or students at coding camp working together on future programming projects.

- ***They are developing a way of independence***

For a few children, departure to camp is their most extended time far away from home. While this isn't always easy (for children and parents), time away will allow a toddler to discover how to make decisions on their own in a new environment. If difficulties come up social or otherwise they'll need to believe in their capacities to seek solutions (with the assistance of camp counsellors, of course). This problem-solving ability also builds confidence and makes children feel empowered.

- ***Self-discovery opportunities***

The sad reality is that being a toddler or adolescent isn't always easy. Problems with bullying or social anxiety can make a day a struggle, surely children. Camp can present a strong shake of faculty difficulties and permit a youth the chance to hamper and obtain a far better sense of who they're. The centre can put students in touch with differing types of individuals that open their eyes to diversity, acceptance, and empathy. In short, the camp experience is often powerful.

Camp can desire a fun, freeing adventure for teenagers. But sometimes, the advantages go even deeper and transcend "fun within the sun." The centre can give children the tools to affect social or intellectual problems, skills which will stick with them for a lifetime. And while we're talking benefits, let's not forget how beneficial a camp is often for busy parents!

What does one want to accomplish together with your camp? What does one want your campers to return away with in terms of enrichment and learning? These are vital considerations as you're employed in designing your camp program.

Having a transparent schedule for the entire summer is vital on multiple levels. It keeps children on task and your camp organized, so there's never wasted time. It also can help children develop skills. For example, maybe you run a music camp and need to schedule basic music theory lessons early within the centre, practice with instruments within the middle, and then a special concert toward the top of the camp. As the centre progresses, children accrue more skills and have an opportunity to point out those skills at the summer's top.

You'll want to schedule everything daily if you've got a more free-form camp without a fine arts or athletics focus. Maybe you begin your days with a fun icebreaker activity, take an excursion within the middle of the day, then have a fun activity, sort of a scavenger hunt later in the day. Again, scheduling the day puts children comfortable. They know what's coming and realize you usually have activities to keep them engaged.

Scheduling the activities at your camp daily, weekly, and monthly is crucial for effective camp management. Building a calendar of events you develop alongside your staff may be a great step toward an organized, enriching camp experience.

CHAPTER TEN

Summer camp activities

One of the major important parts of camp management is thorough planning. Getting into an idea can take the strain off you and your staff and keep the times moving, so campers are always engaged and having fun. And careful scheduling ensures that you're pacing activities appropriately, which makes for a well-functioning camp.

Overall, the opportunities for fun are endless. Does one want your camp to stress art? Sports? Academics? Here are a couple of available games and crafting ideas to urge you were thinking:

- ***Scavenger hunts***

Scavenger hunts are a classic camp activity for a reason. They combine physical activity with problem-solving for a fun competition that tests brains and brawn. And suppose you group campers into pairs or teams. In that case, scavenger hunts also can be an excellent thanks to promote bonding among your campers.

- ***Camp Olympics***

"Olympics" may be a catch-all term for any competition. It doesn't need to be sports, though that's an option. Any tournament that promotes friendly competition among campers may be a good way to motivate campers to move or produce great work.

- ***Tie-dye***

Creating crafts that campers can wear is popular for a reason. Making a hand dye shirt or a friendship bracelet is fun and fool proof. It sends campers home with a memento that they'll treasure for years to return. Crafts also are an excellent idea on those pesky days when the weather isn't cooperating.

- ***Write and perform songs***

If you've got a more performative group of campers, having them add teams to write down a song and then execute it's an excellent thanks to get their creative juices flowing. And if you would like to place a more modern, competitive twist on this, you'll have campers participate during a rap battle.

- ***Relay races***

Are your campers more athletic? Have them compete in relay races. A relay requires teamwork and competition. You'll even have campers make their way through a varied obstacle course so that they must try to do a special activity on different legs of the relay. Introducing that sort of variety can make things a touch more entertaining.

CHAPTER ELEVEN

There are many reasons to travel into the summer with some camp game or crafting ideas. They will be pulled out at a moment's notice to urge your campers to be excited and engaged. And while these are just a couple of pictures, many counsellors enjoy arising with their games which may continue to become classic, signature games at their camps.

- ***Icebreaker ideas***

A camp places several children in a completely new place, surrounded by strangers. Taking children out of their comfort zones is one of the good benefits of a centre. But it takes a while for campers to start feeling those benefits and you'll want to take steps to ensure your trailers are comfortable in their new environment with their new soon-to-be friends. There are quite a few tried-and-true camp icebreakers.

- ***Behaviour modification***

Summer camp offers a replacement sense of freedom and exploration for youngsters. While this is often one of the simplest parts of the centre, it can cause misbehaviour. That's why any centre must possess a clearly defined discipline policy. Your policy should respect the liberty of the camp, treat children fairly, and promote better behaviour for all campers.

- ***Summer camp letters to oldsters***

When it involves sending their child off to camp, parents have concerns. It's your responsibility to keep them within the loop so that they know their child is safe and happy at the centre. One of the simplest ways to speak with your campers' parents is thru a letter. This will be an introductory or regular follow-up letter at the start of camp. Though the term letter might cause you to consider paper, these also can be emailed to oldsters. But what do you have to include in this letter?

- ***A little bit about yourself and your staff***

What are your qualifications? Your experience? Why would you like to open a camp in the first place? Your campers' parents are probably wondering about all of those things. You ought to also introduce your staff. Have your counsellors write a fast blurb about themselves so parents can study counsellors in their own words.

What activities does one have planned? Give a summary of what each day at camp will be like for their children. What games does one have planned? Will children be working in teams or groups? What meals and snacks do one have planned? What about day trips? Details regarding lifestyle at camp will be of interest to oldsters. They can put them comfortable as they send their children off.

- ***Give your contact information***

Parents need how to urge in-tuned with you and your staff. While this may surely be included in other camp materials, it's never a bad idea to remind parents about how they will get in-tuned with you which you welcome regular contact if they ever have questions, concerns, or feedback.

- ***Explain your goals***

What does one want campers to require far away from your camp? You ought to have clear ideas regarding your centre's enrichment opportunities. Outline them at a high level during this letter and explain why the activities and structure you've got planned will assist you in achieving these goals.

- ***Outline some history***

When was this camp started? Are there special traditions at this camp? No, parents don't get to know every little thing about your camp's history. But including a broad overview adds some colour to your letter and provides entertaining context.

- ***Include past testimonials***

If applicable, add some quotes from past campers. Or maybe add feedback from parents of previous campers. This may assist you in in "show" instead of "tell" prospective campers how great your camp is.

CHAPTER TWELVE

Summer camp letters are an excellent thanks to opening up a dialogue with the oldsters of your campers. It sets them comfortable, gives them the knowledge they have, and lets them know you're accessible and approachable. Put care into your letter and proofread it before sending it out.

- ***Summer camp menu planning***

When you collected registrations before camp began, you gathered medical forms that outlined your campers' medical conditions and allergies. These are important when planning your summer camp's menu. Albeit you're running each day camp that gives only a little snack every day, keeping track of your campers' dietary restrictions may be a crucial part of planning. Beyond that, you would like to ensure all your campers have access to delicious, nutritious food that matches their needs.

- ***Find some recipes***

You'll need tons of recipes if you're providing meals for your campers. They'll keep you ready and help your staff know exactly what to try to do when it involves feeding your campers. Specialize in recipes that are fairly easy to form, are often made before time (and then heated up), and may be affordably made in bulk. You furthermore may want meals which will be quickly adjusted to support dietary restrictions and appeal to picky eaters (without serving chicken nuggets every night). Here are a couple of resources which will assist you if you're trying to find camp recipes:

Have an idea for purchasing food: What grocery are you getting to get food from? Having an area like Costco or Walmart that permits you to shop for food in bulk (at affordable prices) is extremely important as you develop your menu.

Prioritize fresh fruit and vegetables: They're delicious and healthy you can't fail. With many vitamins, minerals, and fibre, these options will make campers feel good and show parents that you're providing their children with healthy alternatives.

Emphasize foods that provide energy: Each day at camp sure is often long. That's why it's so important to supply nutrition that gives campers power and many of it. This is often particularly important if you're running a camp centred on sports or physical activity. Foods with protein, like eggs, can give campers the physical energy and brain power they have to tackle the day. Nuts, yoghurt, and fruit also are affordable, energy-giving options. Avoid refined carbs or sugary foods, as this will give campers a quick burst of energy that quickly turns to sluggishness. And it's probably best to avoid caffeine with younger campers.

Have an idea for handling special circumstances: Whether it's a gluten allergy or a spiritual dietary observance, you want to ensure you're prepared for campers' special diets. When preparing food, carefully mark which meals are, for example, peanut-free so that you'll make sure the right meal goes to the proper camper. Prepare these meals before time if possible, as performing on meals at the eleventh hour can cause you to form mistakes. For example, if you've got a camper that keeps kosher, confirm your kitchen is organized so that you'll respect this observance. You don't want your camp to form campers with specific dietary needs feel unwelcome or disrespected.

Make your menu available to oldsters: You would like to be transparent about the food you're serving. That's why it's important to publicize your food, from ingredients to nutritional information. Many camps publish their menu on their website, with a note from the person responsible for culinary services. You'll also send the menu home as a handout (with your contact information) so that parents can stay informed and discuss concerns with you as they are available.

Let's be honest: You can't order pizza for your campers a day. Getting into with a transparent plan and many recipes is the best route toward a fun and delicious time at camp.

CHAPTER THIRTEEN

- **Hygiene and sanitation musts**

Camp can get messy. But when you're running a centre, you're running a business. This suggests you've got to ensure certain hygiene and sanitation standards, so campers stay healthy and cosy. Here are some musts:

Plentiful bathrooms: when nature calls, your staff and campers need options. Ensuring these bathrooms are clean, functional, and stocked with soap, paper towels, and more is additionally vital.

Plumbing inspection: To form sure your bathrooms are functional, hire a plumber to require a glance at your plumbing before camp starts. If there are any problems at your facility, you'll identify and fix them before campers arrive. And it's easy to ditch, but having much-purified water at your camp is significant for cleanliness and hydration. Confirm the plumber looks at the water sometimes, the faucet isn't a clean water source, so you would like to choose a filtration system.

For resident camps and showers: To ensure your campers stay clean at your resident camp, confirm you've got a prescribed time for trailers to require batteries. Have your custodial staff regularly keep these showers clean and stocked with soap and shampoo.

Have a chore chart or hire a janitor: Keeping your camp clean may be a lot for one staffer to try. Some efficient camp staffs have an in-depth chore chart, and everybody pitches in to wash. Some camps even have campers dig in on cleaning to show responsibility, providing them agency over their space. But if it's excessive to stay up with, having a janitor on the premises or a daily cleaning service is beneficial.

Practice proper handwashing: This goes for everybody at camp the staff, the campers, and you. Confirm anyone involved in food preparation is regularly washing, and remind all of your campers to scrub their hands before meals. This limits the spread of germs.

It surely isn't the fun or glamorous part of camp life. Still, proper sanitation is so important for the right functioning of your camp. It all comes back to being proactive and staying organized.

- ***What exactly does one expect of your staff members?***

You would like to form your expectations abundantly clear so that you and your employees are on an equivalent page. A transparent description outlining their roles, tasks, and the skills they'll get to work effectively may be a great jumping-off point.

- ***What exactly does one expect of your staff members?***

You would like to form your expectations abundantly clear so that you and your employees are on an equivalent page. A transparent description outlining their roles, tasks, and the skills they'll get to work effectively may be a great jumping-off point.

You can expand these job descriptions during the appliance and interview process. In your form, you ought to give applicants the prospect to elucidate what they'd bring back to your camp and why their past experiences and skills qualify them for an edge. This may make it easy for you to review applications and other materials beat one place.

It would be best if you determined employee policies so that your staff knows the expected behavior. Clear guidelines, like no drinking or drugs, should be a no-brainer and immediately disqualifying if broken. But you'll also need other policies so that your employees have the tools to safely and appropriately affect the youngsters in your camp safely and appropriately. (Because your hires will work with children, you'll want to run a background check.)

Communicate these policies and put the infrastructure in place so that your employees are conscious of the policies and have agreed to follow them. You'll also get to institute a system that ensures these policies are followed for the duration of the camp.

Another major staffing factor involves salaries: What proportion will you pay your staff members? Will a number of your younger staffers be volunteers? Will staffers who return in subsequent years make quite first-time staff members? These are all inquiries to consider about your budget and profit goals. Ensure most are paid fairly while keeping your business plan in mind.

Why do you have to consider hiring international staff?

You want the simplest possible team for your camp people trained to figure with kids who are respectful, hard-working, and hooked into providing an excellent time for all campers.

CONCLUSION

You should always examine and change your plans on a regular basis, no matter how far in advance you plan. These are living documents, and you should adapt your strategies when the external and internal climates change. It is generally advisable to incorporate all of your stakeholders in the planning process. For example, if you are creating an activity plan and camp schedules, include your staff who will be carrying out those activities in the planning process. Lack of planning will always be evident, so remember that putting in the extra effort upfront in planning can make your job easier, operations smoother, and overall camps better in the long term.